Save Me, Smee!

Written by Melinda LaRose

Illustrated by Character Building Studio and the Disney Storybook Artists

Disney PRESS

New York • Los Angeles

Ahoy, mateys! Do you want to join my pirate crew? Then just say the pirate password, "Yo-ho-ho!" As part of my crew, you'll need to learn the Never Land pirate pledge.

TODAY'S PIRATE PLEDGE

A pirate is always willing to help out a friend.

"**B**last it, Smee! I didn't sleep a wink all night," says Hook. "Captain Cuddly is missing! You know I can't go beddy-bye without my teddy bear."

Just then, Hook spots a teeny, tiny treasure chest.

"Why, it's me first treasure chest from when I was just a wee little pirate."

There's a treasure map inside the chest!

"We have to go across Slippery Snake River through Crumble Canyon. Then X marks the spot at—gulp!—Skull Rock," says Smee. "Those are the most perilous places in all of Never Land."

"So what?" says Hook. "There's treasure and I want it."

"Be careful, Mr. Smee," says Jake. "You're heading for Slippery Snake River!"

Smee nods. "I'm afraid the Captain's after treasure."

"We could follow in case there's any trouble," says Izzy.

"Oh, you sea pups are so kind," says Smee.

Trouble is Captain Hook's middle name!

"Danger, schmanger," says Hook. "It's just a river."
Hook jumps on the back of a slippery snake.

BOING, BOING, SPLASH!

"Save me, Smee!" calls the Captain.

"Oh dear, oh dear! Right away, Cap'n!"

BOING, BOING, SPLASH! Smee falls into the river, too!

"We have to help Hook and Smee," says Jake.

"But how can we get to them?" asks Cubby. "The snakes are too slippery to jump across!"

What did the snake say when he learned to ride a bike?

"We'd better think of something quick," says Jake.

Izzy makes a lasso and tosses it to Smee. "Mr. Smee,
catch!" she calls.

Then Jake and the crew pull Smee and Hook to shore.

"Great work, Iz," says Jake.

"Thank you, sea pups," whispers Smee.

"See? That wasn't dangerous at all," says Hook as he staggers to the shore and falls down.

"Oh, my," says Smee. "What do you say we go back to the Jolly Roger now, Cap'n? I'll make you a nice cup of tea."

"Never!" says Hook. "Crumble Canyon awaits!"

Look, Ma, no hands!

"**CRACKERS!** Hook and Smee are going across that narrow pass," says Skully.

"Be ready to lend a hand, crew," says Jake.

"See, Smee? This is a breeze," says Captain Hook. "I don't even know why they call it Crumble Canyon."

"Well, sir," says Smee, "it's because the sides of the canyon tend to . . ."

"A**IIEEEE**!" yells Hook as the ground beneath him collapses.

" . . . crumble," finishes Smee.

"Save me, Smee!" yells Hook.

"I gotcha, Cap'n," says Smee.

"But who has *you?*" asks Hook.

"Ahh!" Smee starts to fall over the edge of the canyon.

Skully swoops in and grabs Smee.

"I got you, Skully," calls Cubby.

"And I've got *you*," says Izzy.

"Come on, crew! Heave ho! Heave ho!" calls Jake.

Together, they hoist Hook and Smee to safety.

"Are you . . . okay . . . sir?" Smee pants.

"I'll be better when I have that treasure," says Hook.

"Are you sure you don't want to go home? I'll make hot
chocolate with those little marshmallows you like so much."

"I do love little marshmallows," says Hook, "but Skull Rock
and treasure await!"

"Hook can't go to Skull Rock," says Cubby. "It's way too dangerous."

"He'll never give up looking for that treasure," says Smee.

"Unless," says Izzy, "there was an even *better* treasure for him to find."

What do you call a pirate who lives in the mountains?

"Great idea, Iz," says Jake. "We can make a new treasure for Hook to find. Somewhere nice and safe."

"But we don't have any treasure," says Cubby.

"I know where there's a treasure that the Cap'n will just love," says Smee.

"Skully, send word to Sharky and Bones to prepare the treasure," says Jake.

"AYE-AYE!" Skully says.

"Cubby, can you make a new map?" Jake asks.

"AYE-AYE, JAKE!" says Cubby.

Lost!

"Now to get Hook to take the bait," says Jake. "Hey, Izzy," he says loudly enough for Hook to hear. "I can't believe we found a map to the most awesome treasure in all of Never Land!"

"Yeah. Lucky Captain Hook isn't around to take our map to the really awesome treasure," says Izzy.

"Ha! You can't fool the great Captain Hook. I'll be taking the map *and* the treasure," says Hook.

"AW, COCONUTS," says Cubby, winking at Smee. "You tricked us again."

"We'll never find the awesome treasure now," says Skully.

"I don't believe me eyes," says Hook. "The treasure is aboard the Jolly Roger!"

"Oh, is that so?" asks Smee innocently.

"The most awesome treasure in all of Never Land—right on me own ship," says Hook happily.

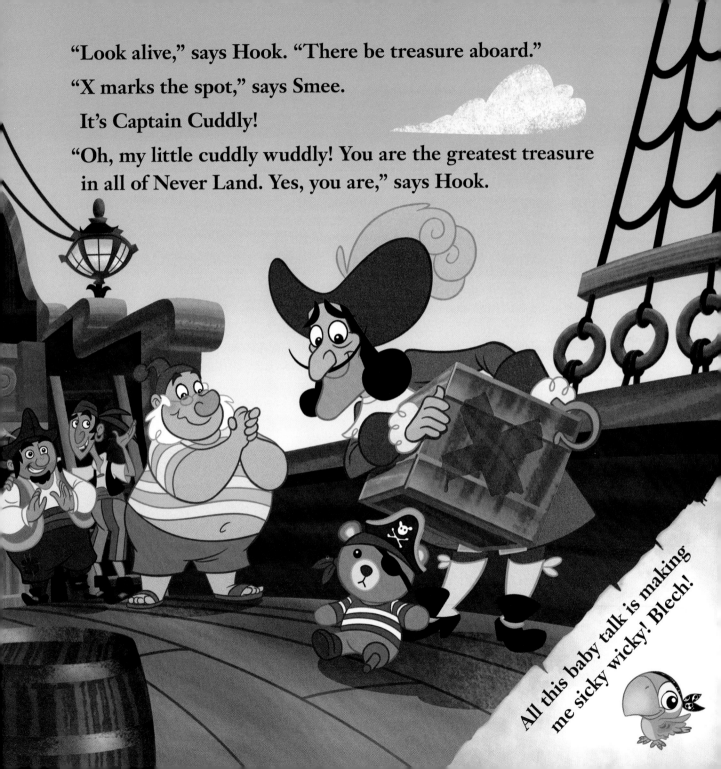

"Look alive," says Hook. "There be treasure aboard."

"X marks the spot," says Smee.

It's Captain Cuddly!

"Oh, my little cuddly wuddly! You are the greatest treasure in all of Never Land. Yes, you are," says Hook.

All this baby talk is making me sicky wicky! Blech!

"He had a little rip," says Bones, "but I fixed him right up."

"Did you have an ouchy, Captain Cuddly?" asks Hook.

"Whew!" says Smee. "Now that we're home, I imagine you won't be needing any more rescuing today, Cap'n."

"Rescuing? What do you mean rescuing?" says Hook. "The great Captain Hook has never needed to be rescued. Isn't that right, Captain Cuddly?"

SPLASH! Hook accidentally knocks his bear overboard.

"Bear overboard!" yells Hook. He dives into the water . . . and finds his bear in the arms of the Tick Tock Croc!

"Save me, Smee! And Captain Cuddly, too!"

"Right away, Cap'n," Smee says as he jumps into the water.